Strawberry Shortcake at the Beach

Grosset & Dunlap

Strawberry Shortcake™ © 2003 Those Characters From Cleveland, Inc.
Used under license by Penguin Group (USA) Inc. All rights reserved.
Published by Grosset & Dunlap, a division of Penguin Young Readers Group,
345 Hudson Street, New York, NY 10014. GROSSET & DUNLAP is a trademark of
Penguin Group (USA) Inc. Published simultaneously in Canada. Printed in China.

ISBN 0-448-43187-4   A B C D E F G H I J

Special Markets ISBN 0-448-43706-6

Strawberry Shortcake at the Beach

By Megan E. Bryant
Illustrated by SI Artists

Grosset & Dunlap • New York

One bright, sunny morning, Strawberry Shortcake woke up and looked out the window. "It's a berry perfect beach day!" she exclaimed. "Wake up, Apple Dumplin'!"

"Beach?" asked Apple Dumplin' sleepily.

"That's right! We're going to Seaberry Beach today with all of our friends," Strawberry said.

They quickly packed everything they would need: two
fluffy towels, sunblock, a yummy picnic lunch, and all of
their beach toys.

"I can't forget these!" Strawberry Shortcake told Apple.
"My new sunglasses!" She put them on, and they were
ready to go.

"Hi, Strawberry!" Huck called as Strawberry walked up to her friends at their meeting place.

"Hi, everybody," Strawberry said.

"Wow! Those sunglasses are great, Strawberry!" Angel Cake said. "Can I try them on?"

"Sure," Strawberry Shortcake replied. "You can borrow them for the day if you want. Just be berry careful with them, please."

"I will," promised Angel.

"Thanks!"

Soon the kids arrived at Seaberry Beach. They went straight to their favorite spot near the lifeguard station and laid out their beach towels.

"Hold still, Apple," said Strawberry Shortcake. Her little sister giggled and squirmed while Strawberry put sunblock on her.

"Let's play catch!" Huck said, getting out his beach ball. The friends made a large circle and played ball.

"It's too hot to play ball anymore," Strawberry Shortcake said to her friends. "Who wants to go in the water?" she asked.

"Me!" shouted everybody at once.

"Don't forget to stay with your buddy," Strawberry reminded her friends. Holding hands, they all raced down to the ocean. The friends laughed and splashed as they played in the water.

"The waves are getting bigger," Strawberry Shortcake said to Orange Blossom. "Do you think that Angel and Ginger are too far out?"

"Maybe," Orange said. She looked a little worried.

"Hey, Ginger! Angel!" Huck yelled. But the waves were crashing so loudly that the girls could barely hear him. Angel turned around to wave to her friends.

Suddenly, a big wave knocked her down!

Angel slowly sat up, wiping the salty water out of her eyes.

"Angel! Angel!" her friends called as they ran over to her. They helped her to her feet.

"Did you get hurt?" Strawberry asked.

"No, I'm okay," said Angel Cake.

"Whoa, Angel, that wave was huge!" Huck said. "You have to be careful not to turn your back on the ocean when you play in the water!"

"I think she knows that now," said Strawberry Shortcake with a smile as she took a piece of seaweed off of Angel's hat.

"Well, let's go have our picnic!" said Orange Blossom.
"I'm really hungry!"

Suddenly, Angel Cake felt something snap beneath her
foot. She looked down, and her hands flew to her face.

Oh, no! she thought. I broke Strawberry's sunglasses!

Angel Cake held the broken glasses tightly as she trudged up the sand after her friends.

"Would you like some of these sweet, juicy strawberries from my garden?" Strawberry Shortcake asked. "They're berry delicious!"

I can't tell Strawberry about her sunglasses now, Angel thought miserably. *It will ruin her whole day.*

"No thanks, I'm not very hungry," Angel said, trying to smile.

As soon as she got a chance, Angel hid the sunglasses in her bag. *I'll tell Strawberry later,* Angel promised herself.

After the picnic, the friends built sand castles and played tag. Finally, it was time to go home.

"Bye, everybody!" Strawberry said to her friends. Then she turned to Angel. "Can I have my sunglasses back, please?"

Angel opened her mouth to tell Strawberry that the glasses were broken, but the words wouldn't come out. Instead she said, "Um, can I give them back tomorrow?"

"Sure," Strawberry said with a smile. "See you then!"

At home, Angel felt worse and worse about the broken sunglasses. She stroked her pet lamb's fleecy wool.

"Why didn't I just tell Strawberry that I broke her sunglasses?" she said to Vanilla Icing. "Now I've only made things worse! What if she won't be my friend anymore?"

Angel Cake sighed. "I don't know what to do. Maybe I should ask Ginger Snap for advice. She's good at fixing things."

"Hi, Angel Cake. Come in," said Ginger Snap. "What are you doing here?"

"I have a problem," said Angel sadly. She showed Ginger the broken sunglasses and explained what had happened. "I shouldn't have worn them in the water. Strawberry asked me to be careful! I'm afraid she'll be really mad."

"That is a tough problem," Ginger said.
"But Angel, it was an accident. Just tell her
you're sorry. I'm sure she'll understand. And
if you go tell her now, you won't have to worry
about it anymore. I can come with you if you want."

"Yes, please," said Angel. She wasn't looking forward
to telling Strawberry, but already she felt a little better.

A few minutes later, Angel and Ginger knocked on Strawberry's front door.

"Hello!" said Strawberry Shortcake. "This is a berry nice surprise!"

"Strawberry, I have something to tell you," Angel Cake said in a soft voice. She took a deep breath and pulled the broken sunglasses out of her pocket. "When that big wave knocked me down at the beach, your sunglasses fell off my face. Then I stepped on them by accident and they broke. I'm really, really sorry. And I'm also sorry that I didn't tell you when it happened. Are you mad at me?"

"No, I'm not mad at you," Strawberry said to Angel Cake. "I know you didn't mean to break the sunglasses. It's okay."

"Really?" asked Angel

"Of course!" Strawberry replied. "The important thing is that you didn't get hurt when the wave knocked you down. That matters a lot more than the sunglasses!" Strawberry gave Angel a big hug.

Strawberry Shortcake looked at the sunglasses. "It's too bad they broke, though," she said. "They were my berry favorite sunglasses. Oh, well—I guess I'll just throw them away."

"Wait a minute," said Ginger Snap. "I have an idea!" She reached into her toolbox and pulled out a tube of glue. Ginger picked up the broken sunglasses. "A drop of glue here, a drop of glue there . . .   good as new!"

"Oh, Ginger, thank you berry much
for fixing my sunglasses!" Strawberry said.

"Thank you for fixing *everything!*" Angel Cake said to Ginger.

"You're welcome!" Ginger said. "I love to fix things
for my friends!"